ROTHERHAM PUBLIC LIBRARIES

I WANT A CAT

Tony Ross

Andersen Press · London

British Library Cataloguing in Publication Data
Ross, Tony, 1938
    I want a cat.
    I. Title
    823'.914[J]

    ISBN 0-86264-237-X

© 1989 by Tony Ross
First published in Great Britain by Andersen Press Ltd., 20 Vauxhall
Bridge Road, London SW1V 2SA. Published in Australia by
Random Century Australia Pty., Ltd., 20 Alfred Street,
Milsons Point, Sydney, NSW 2061. All rights reserved.
Colour separated in Switzerland by Photolitho AG, Gossau, Zürich.
Printed and bound in Italy by Grafiche AZ, Verona.

3   4   5   6   7   8   9

Jessy wanted a cat.

All her friends had pets.

Some of them had big pets and some of them
had little pets.
Jessy felt that she was the *only* girl in the world
with *no* pet…

And Jessy wanted a cat!

Her mum and dad always said, "NO!"
(Crawly, creepy, yowly things, they called them.)
So they kept giving Jessy toy cats instead.

But Jessy wanted a real cat.

Then...Jessy planned a wonderful plan.
She collected lots of fluffy white cloth, some
needles and cotton, and locked herself in
her room.

And she made herself a cat suit.

Next she took all of her proper clothes, and
buried them in the garden.
"I'm going to be the cat in this house," she
purred.

"What on earth do you think you're doing?"
said Mum.

"I'm going to be like this until I get a cat!" said
Jessy. "And if I *don't* get a cat, then I'm going to
be like this for *ever*!"

On Monday Jessy went to school.
When the teacher saw her cat suit, he shouted so
loudly, she jumped up on top of the blackboard,

and wouldn't come down, even for a saucer
of milk.

On Tuesday, Jessy went to a restaurant.
"Cats don't sit at tables," said Jessy. "Even in posh places."

"Milk and trout," she said to the waiter, "and please don't cook the trout. May it be served down here?"

"Certainly, madam," said the waiter.

Soon Jessy began to smell of fish.

When it was time for bath and bed, Dad went to catch Jessy.
"Now you'll *have* to take that silly suit off," he grinned.

"No I won't," said Jessy. "Not until I get a cat."

Then Jessy curled up on her bedroom floor.

In the middle of the night, Mum and Dad were
roused by a horrible noise. It was like a million
pigs falling downstairs, and the neighbours
banging on the front door.

It was Jessy, on the garden wall.
"I WANT A CAT!" she was howling.

"Give her a cat," complained Mr Biggs from
next door.
"Give her a cat," complained Mr Figgs.
"Shouldn't be allowed," complained Mrs Figgs.
"Give her a cat," complained Mum.

So, early next morning, Dad went down to the
pet shop, and chose a cat. He took it to Jessy's
door, and knocked.

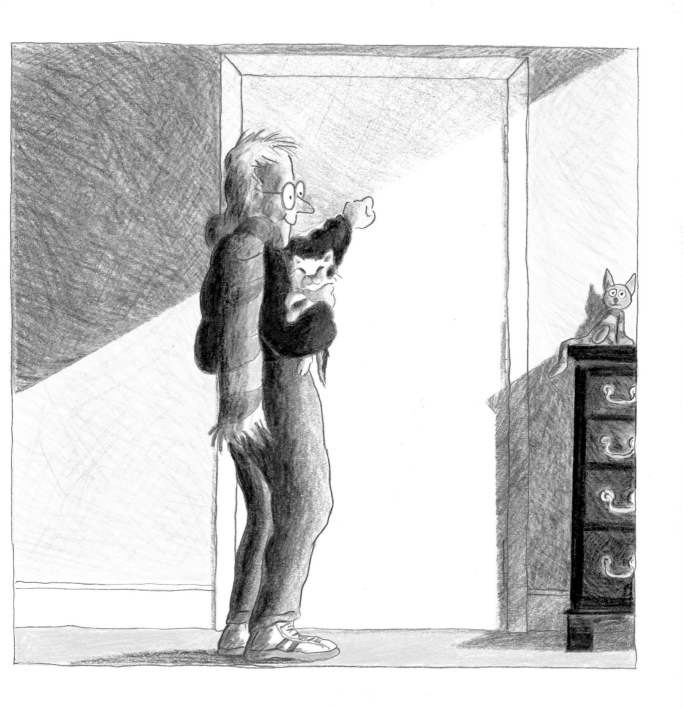

"Jessy," he called, "I've got a surprise for you."

"WOOF! WOOF!" said Jessy, "I WANT..."